This
Dora the Explorer
Annual
belongs to

....

....

Annual 2009

Contents

EGMONT

We bring stories to life

First published in Great Britain 2008 by Egmont UK Limited
239 Kensington High Street, London W8 6SA
Created for Egmont by John Brown Publishing Group
Edited by William Petty • Designed by Jilly Slattery
© 2008 Viacom International Inc.
All rights reserved.
Nickelodeon, Nick Jr., Dora the Explorer and all related titles, logos
and characters are trademarks of Viacom International Inc.

ISBN 978 1 4052 3912 7
3 5 7 9 10 8 6 4 2
Printed in Italy

¡Hola! I'm Dora. I've been reading a fairy story to my friend, Boots. Guess which famous fairy tale it was!

Was it the Three Little Dogs?

Was it the Three Little Pigs?

Or was it the Three Little Frogs?

8

Next?

Well done, it was the Three Little Pigs! In the story, the cleverest pig builds his house of bricks so the Big Bad Wolf can't get in.

Let's use our imagination, and make up the rest of the story! A king wants the Pigs to go and fetch his mummy, who is far away. But the Pigs are too scared to go!

9

Don't worry, we'll go! Map says we have to go to the Three Bears' House, then around the Beanstalk to get to the Rainbow – that's where we'll find the King's mummy. Let's go! ¡Vámonos!

Hurry, hurry, the King's all alone!
Let's get the King's mummy
and bring her back home!

Here's the Three Bears' Cottage. Look, someone has eaten a bowl of porridge and broken a chair. It's Goldilocks! Oh no, the Bears are back. They'll be cross when they see what's happened. Let's imagine ...

... The Bears are happy to see us! They love having visitors and don't mind about the porridge. Let's help them fix the chair by choosing the right length leg.

Tick the leg that's just right!

a

b

c

11

Now let's find the Beanstalk. Look, there's Jack. He's got a golden egg. Uh-oh, I think I hear the Giant coming. He'll be cross that Jack stole his egg. Let's imagine ...

The Giant is a nice giant! He's not cross at all, and he's got more golden eggs for Jack. Oh no, he dropped them! Don't worry Giant, we'll find the golden eggs!

How many golden eggs are there? Write in the answer!

13

We did it, now let's find the Rainbow.
Oh no - a fierce dragon! Let's imagine ...
She's turned into a friendly dragon!
But she's hurt her foot.

Let's find something in Backpack to stick
on her foot. Now what can we give her
as a sweet reward for being so brave?

Tick what
we need.

14

The dragon took us over the Rainbow. Look, there's the King's mummy! She says she misses him, and wants to go home with us. Let's go! ¡Vámonos!

We did it, we brought the King's mummy home! They're very pleased to see each other. Thanks for helping! ¡Gracias!

WE DID IT! ¡LO HICIMOS!

Rainbow Maze

We need to get over the rainbow! Will you show the dragon the way? Watch out for the clouds!

Start

Do you see Benny? Wave to him!

Finish

17

Fairy Land

Dont let Swiper swipe the King's crown. Say "Swiper, no swiping" three times.

Dora and Boots are on an adventure in Fairy Land. Pretend you're in Fairy Land too - what would you like to do?

Put a tick beside these fairy tale characters when you find them!

Stuck Truck

¡Hola! I'm in Boots' bedroom. He is showing me all his trucks. He loves trucks!

This is 10-wheeler.

This is Bulldozer.

This is Crane.

This is Rojo the fire truck.

This is Tow-truck.

And this is Ice Cream Truck!

Uh-oh, it sounds like a truck is in trouble! Can you see which one it is?

That's right, Ice Cream Truck is in trouble! He's stuck in a ditch near Play Park!

Don't worry, we'll get him out! Let's ask Map where to go. He says we need to go over Puzzle Bridge and across Crocodile Lake to get to Play Park. Let's go! ¡Vámonos!

21

Ew, mud! We need a truck with lots of wheels to drive us through the mud. Which truck shall we call?

TICK A TRUCK!

That's right, 10-wheeler will drive us across. Here he is! Wait, do you hear Swiper? He'll try to swipe 10-wheeler's wheels. Oh no, it's too late! He threw them away.

SWIPER, NO SWIPING!

Don't worry 10-wheeler, we'll find your wheels. We need to count 10 wheels we can use.

Circle the 2 flat tyres which we can't use!

We did it! 10-wheeler drove us to Puzzle Bridge. But there are pieces missing. We need a truck who can lift things to help us. Which truck shall we call?

TICK A TRUCK!

That's right, Crane can help – she loves lifting things! We need to match the missing pieces to the holes to fix the bridge.

We fixed the bridge, and we made it to Crocodile Lake. We need a truck with a long ladder to lift us over the crocodiles. Which truck shall we call?

TICK A TRUCK!

24

Right, Rojo the fire truck! He has a long ladder! He'll lift us over the crocodiles. Thanks, Rojo. ¡Gracias!

Look, I see Ice Cream Truck. To get him out, we need a truck with a big hook. Which truck shall we call?

TICK A TRUCK!

Right, Tow-truck! Here he comes. Uh-oh, I hear Swiper the fox! He'll try to swipe Tow-truck's hook! Say 'Swiper, no swiping!' three times!

SWIPER, NO SWIPING!

PULL!

We did it, we stopped Swiper! Now we need to get Ice Cream Truck out. Will you help us pull the chain? Put your hands in front of you and pull the chain. Pull!

We did it, we rescued Ice Cream Truck from the ditch. He's not stuck any more! Now he can take ice cream to Play Park. Thanks for helping! ¡Gracias!

WE DID IT!
¡LO HICIMOS!

27

What's Changed?

These pictures look the same, but 10 things are different in picture 2. Spot them all!

1

At Play Park

What's happening at Play Park? When you see a picture, say the word out loud!

 Isa

 Swiper

 Boots

 Ice Cream Truck

 strawberry

 ice cream

 banana

 chocolate

After and I rescued  from the ditch, we went to Play Park to give everyone . Do you like ? I like it a lot! My favourite flavour is . Who else wants an ?  would like an . Her favourite flavour is . Uh-oh,

I hear . He'll try to swipe the !

To stop him, say ', no swiping!'

three times. We did it, we stopped !

Thanks for helping! would like an

 too. Can you guess what his favourite

flavour is? Right - it's !

What's your favourite flavour?

31

Pinto the Pony Express

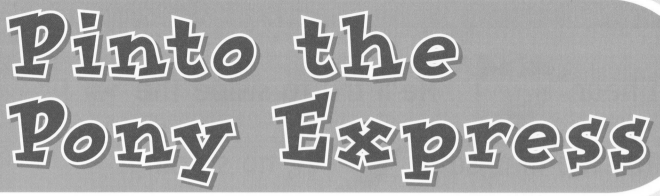

¡Hola! This this is Pinto. He's one fast pony! Val the octopus wants us to deliver a special package of cowboy cookies to Benny the bull. But we need to watch out for Swiper - he likes cowboy cookies, too.

Let's ask Map where to go to deliver the cookies. He says we need to go through the Gold Tunnel and through Rattlesnake Rocks to get to Benny's Barn. Let's go! ¡Vámonos!

That cactus is moving. Oh no, it's Swiper the fox! He'll swipe the cookies! Say 'Swiper, no swiping!' three times to stop him.

SWIPER, NO SWIPING!

¡Excelente! **Great!** We stopped Swiper. Now we're at the Gold Tunnel. Look, it's Isa. She says it's very dark in the tunnel.

Help me find something in Backpack that will help us see in the dark!

Tick what we need.

34

That's right, a lantern will help us see in the dark. Let's go through the Gold Tunnel. Isa says we need to follow the seven gold stones. Count seven gold stones with me! And there's the way out.

Now we need to get through the Rattlesnake Rocks. Will you help us? Say 'para' to make Pinto stop when you see a rattlesnake. ¡Para! Stop!

We made it through Rattlesnake Rocks. Now let's take the cookies to Benny. Wow, Pinto sure is fast. Uh-oh, we're heading for the edge of the cliff. Say 'para' to make Pinto stop. ¡Para! Stop!

TWIRL!

Oh no, the cookies went flying! I know, I can catch them with my silver lasso. I need your help. Put your arm in the air and twirl your lasso. Twirl!

We did it, we saved the cookies! Thanks for helping. ¡Gracias! Remember, we need to look out for Swiper. Do you see that sneaky fox? There he is! Say 'Swiper, no swiping!' three times!

SWIPER, NO SWIPING!

We stopped Swiper, thanks for helping! Now we're at Benny's Barn. Hi Benny, we brought you some cowboy cookies. Benny's very excited.

Uh-oh, I hear Swiper the fox! Say 'Swiper, no swiping!' three times to stop him. ¡Excelente! Great! We did it – we stopped Swiper! Now Benny will share the cookies with us!

SWIPER, NO SWIPING!

Find a star cookie for Dora. Find a boot for Boots. Find a hat for Benny. Find a horseshoe for Pinto. Is there one left over?

There is one left over - the cactus! Swiper the fox really likes cowboy cookies. Let's give it to him. Here you are, Swiper! We took Benny his cookies. Thanks for helping! *¡Gracias!*

WE DID IT! *¡LO HICIMOS!*

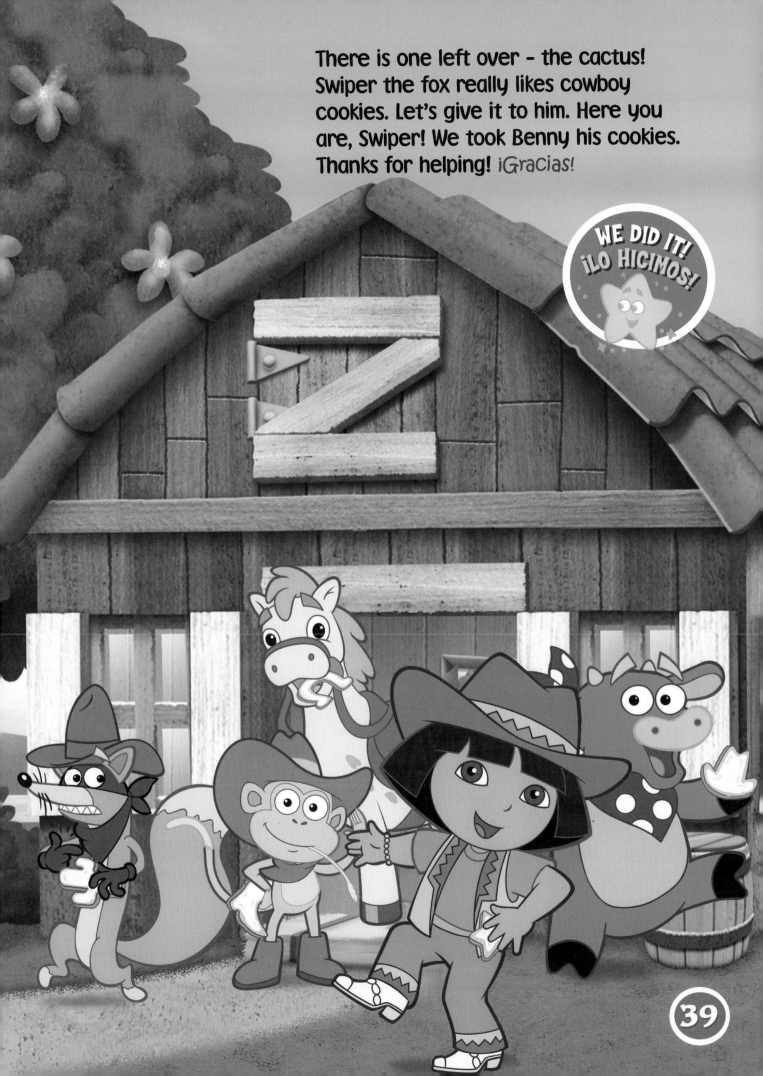

Rocky Road

Will you help us find a way through Rattlesnake Rocks? Watch out for rattlesnakes!

Start

How many snakes are there? Write in the answer.

Finish

41

Cowboy Puzzles

Only one shadow matches the cactus by Boots. Which one is it?

1 **2** **3** **4** **5**

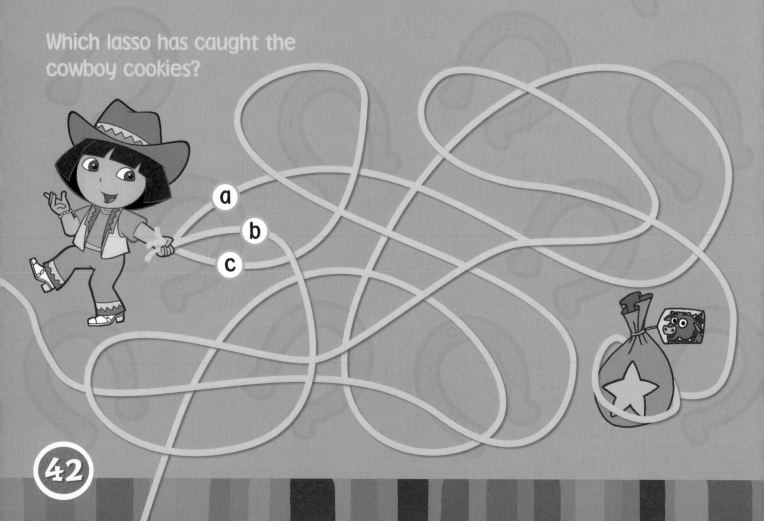

Which lasso has caught the cowboy cookies?

a **b** **c**

Make a Cookie!

Do you like cowboy cookies? Draw your favourite cookie shape here, and decorate it!

Mmmm! I love cookies!

Little Star

¡Hola! It's night time. Boots and I are going to make a wish on Little Star up in the sky.

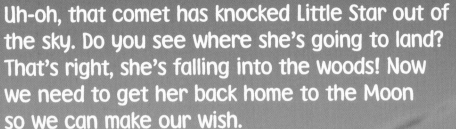

Uh-oh, that comet has knocked Little Star out of the sky. Do you see where she's going to land? That's right, she's falling into the woods! Now we need to get her back home to the Moon so we can make our wish.

Don't worry Little Star, we'll get you home to the Moon! Let's ask Map where to go. He says we need to go over Troll Bridge and past Tico's Tree to get to Tall Mountain. Let's go! ¡Vámonos!

45

Look, it's Troll Bridge. I hope we don't run into that Grumpy Old Troll. Do you see him?

That's right, there he is under the bridge! Let's ask him if we can cross to the other side.

The Troll says we need to solve his riddle before we cross his bridge. Read the pictures and say the riddle out loud with us!

 light, bright,
Can you see the ✨ so bright?
 light, bright,
How many ✨ are there tonight?

OK, we need to count all the stars. Will you help us? Tell us how many you see.

1, 2, 3, 4, 5, 6, 7, 8, 9, 10. I see 10 stars. Oh no, the Grumpy Old Troll says we missed one on the ground!

How many stars are there? Write in the answer!

We forgot to count the brightest star of them all – Little Star! That means there are 11 stars. Now we can cross Troll Bridge. Let's go! ¡Vámonos!

Here's Tico's Tree. And here's Tico. Wait, do you hear Swiper? He'll try to swipe Little Star! If you see him, shout 'Swiper, no swiping!' three times.

SWIPER, NO SWIPING!

We were too late. Swiper swiped Little Star! Do you see where Swiper hid Little Star?

Don't worry, Tico will go and get Little Star.
Go, Tico! ¡Anda, Tico! Let's help Tico get to Little Star.

Hooray! Tico saved Little Star from
the tree. Thanks for your help, too!
Where do we need to go next?

Now, we need to go to Tall Mountain and get Little Star back home to the Moon. Let's go! ¡Vámonos!

THROW!

We made it to the top of Tall Mountain! Little Star is almost home! Will you help us throw Little Star back up to the Moon? 1 ... 2 ... 3 ... THROW! ¡Tira!

We did it ¡Lo hicimos!, we got Little Star back home to the Moon. Thanks for your help! And now everyone can make a wish. What will you wish for? I hope all your wishes come true!

Star Puzzles

Only two stars are the same shape. Tick them!

Grumpy Old troll has got a riddle for us! What's the answer? Think about it.

What can run, but can't walk?

A Baby

A Chicken

Water

A House

Make a Wish

Would you like to make a wish on Little Star?
Draw what you wish for here!

I hope your wish comes true!

Star Spotting!

We're making a wish on Little Star! These pictures look the same, but 10 things are different in picture 2. Spot them all!

1

Journey to the Purple Planet

¡Hola! Boots and I are looking up at outer space. Boots says he'd love to meet someone from space. Hey, look! A flying saucer!

It's landing over here. Wow, little space creatures! They say their names are Flinky, Inky, Plinky, Dinky and Al. I'm Dora! ¡Soy Dora!

Oh no, their spaceship broke. Now they're sad because they can't get home to the Purple Planet.

57

Don't worry, we'll help you get home. Map says we have to go past the Space Rocks and through the Milky Way to get to the Purple Planet.

But first we need a rocket. Isa has one. Isa, can we borrow your rocket? It's really important. She says we can. Let's go! ¡Vámonos!

58

Let's count down to blast off. Count with us! 10, 9, 8, 7, 6, 5, 4, 3, 2, 1, BLAST OFF! Now let's take Flinky, Inky, Plinky, Dinky and Al home to the Purple Planet.

We've arrived at the Space Rocks. We mustn't hit them! Say '¡Arriba!' to make the rocket go up so we don't hit the Space Rocks. ¡Arriba!

We made it to the Milky Way. But it's very hard to see through it! Let's follow the stars. Will you help us?

Draw over the star outline to see what shape it makes.

Thanks for your help! Hmm, I think the aliens are hungry. Let's have some food. Do you see a floating hotdog? Point to a space cookie! Where's the orange?

¡Mmm, delicioso! **Delicious!**
Ooh, a comet. Comets go really fast. I know, let's hitch a ride.
Wheeeeeee!

We did it! ¡Lo hicimos!
Thanks for helping. Uh-oh, we
need to change a battery in
the rocket. Don't let Swiper
the fox swipe it. Say 'Swiper,
no swiping!' three times.

SWIPER,
NO SWIPING!

Thanks for helping us stop
Swiper. Now we need to land.
Which one is the Purple Planet?

Tick the
Purple Planet!

Here we are on the Purple Planet. Everything's purple - the Purple Planet is cool! Flinky, Inky, Plinky, Dinky and Al are so glad to be home again. Great work!

WE DID IT!
¡LO HICIMOS!

63

Space Rocks!

Start

Help us find a way through the Space Rocks. Make sure you don't hit any!

Don't let Swiper swipe the rocket. Say "Swiper, no swiping" three times.

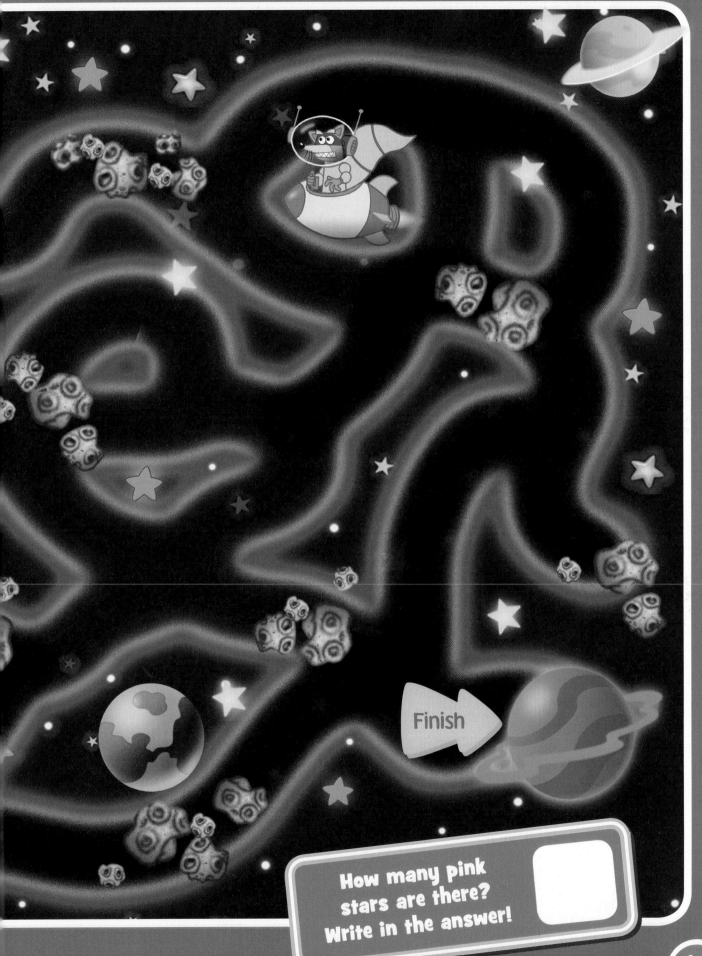

Finish

How many pink stars are there? Write in the answer!

65

Floating in Space

Move your arms and
swim through space with
Dora and Boots! How
many planets are there?

Tick these
space things when
you find them!

Answers

Page 7 The 10 bananas are on pages 11, 19, 22, 27, 30, 31, 34, 36, 41 and 51.

Page 11 Leg b is just right to fix the chair.

Page 13 There are 9 golden eggs.

Page 14 We need plasters and a lollipop for the dragon.

Pages 16-17

Page 23 These wheels have flat tyres so can't be used.

Page 24

Pages 28-29

Page 34 We need the lantern.

Page 40 There are 6 snakes.

Page 42 Shadow 4 matches the cactus. Lasso b has caught the cookies.

Page 48 Little Star is hidden in the tree.

Page 49

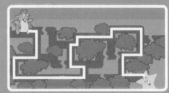

Page 52 These stars are the same.

Water can run, but not walk.

Page 54

Page 60 The stars make a teddy bear shape.

Page 62 This is the Purple Planet.

Pages 64-65 There are 8 pink stars.

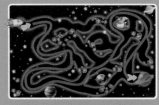

Page 66 There are 5 planets (including the Purple Planet)

Have you seen the Dora Magazine?

FREE Bug rescue game!

WIN! FANTASTIC DORA PRIZES!

NICK JR.

DORA the EXPLORER™

Issue 34

ON SALE every 3 weeks!

FREE fabulous gift every issue!

NICK JR DORA the EXPLORER

©2007 Viacom

Bursting with Dora adventures!

We bring stories to life

EGMONT

Join Dora in her exciting adventures with this fantastic magazine from Egmont

Packed full of

✸ Adventures ✸ Great stories ✸ Games ✸ Colouring

Available in all good retailers now!